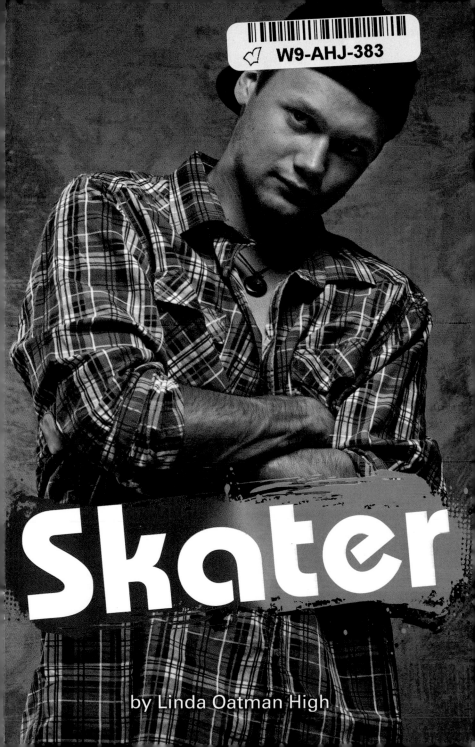

Skater

by Linda Oatman High

ISBN-13: 978-1-68021-153-5
ISBN-10: 1-68021-153-6
eBook: 978-1-63078-485-0

Printed in Guangzhou, China
NOR/1115/CA21501590

20 19 18 17 16   1 2 3 4 5

"Don't be a hater!
For sure I can
be a skater."

I say this
to my sister.
Her name is Kate.

She frowns.
Looks down.
Rolls her eyes.

No surprise.
I am her
little brother.

With one leg
shorter
than
the other.

Mom **believes** in me.
Dad
believes in me.

9

My sister
calls me lame.
She calls me limpy.
Or gimpy.
And she says I'm
wimpy.

Kids at school
say I'm cool.
But I'm no fool.
They call me
lame
behind my back.
Maybe they tell
jokes too.

I'm no good
on ball courts.

I can't
play school
sports.

But I'll show Kate.
I'll show those
who hate.

I will skate.

I **save**
my money.

"Josh, honey,"
says Mom.
"Why are
you working
so hard? Your
gas station
job is
too much.
Maybe you need
a break."

"No, thanks," I say.

"I have a goal.
I'm saving
my money.
I want to buy
a skateboard."

Mom nods.
"Go for it," she says.
"You will be
a rad skater."

Dad grins.
"Dream big," he says.
"I dig the idea
of you skating."

"OMG,"
says Kate.
"Sweet."
But it is
fake.

She doesn't
think I'm
for real.
Because
I'm the
little brother.

With one leg
shorter
than
the other.

I work and work.
And save and save.
By April
I have enough money.

I buy
the board.

It is cool blue
with red
flames.
I put my name
on the bottom.

"Oh my gosh, Josh!" says Mom. "That rocks."

"Jump on it.
Just soar!"
says Dad.

"Looks like a bore to me," says Kate. All she does is watch TV.

I
think
she
is jealous.

I'm at the

skate park

every night.
I skate
until the day
fades
to dark.
Sometimes
longer.

Under the stars.
Under the moon.

I skate from April
to June.

I see
a sign
at school.

X-Treme Skate!

July 9
City Skate Park
Be There
Or Be Square

"Dude," says a girl
near me.
"Not to be rude.
But can you
really ride
a board?"

"Like anybody else,"
I say.
"With practice.
All you have to do is try.
Spread your wings. Fly.
Be brave.
Don't care what people say."

ATE PARK
IERE
E SQUARE

"Okay," says the girl.
Then she just
walks away.

July 9.
My big day
to skate.

Kids
wait in line.
It goes
far down
the sidewalk.
So many
other
skaters.

I take a deep breath.
This is not life
or death.

It is my turn.
I'm going to burn
up the ramp.
I have
cool
moves.

I'm in
the zone.
Grooving to my
own
beat.

I do flips.
Slides.
Grabs.
I hang ten.
Catch air.
Don't care
if anybody stares.

I win a trophy.
It is gold.

Mom cries.

Dad wipes his eyes.

Kate looks shocked.

"You are a great skater!"

My sister
is not
a hater.

I am
a
skater.

TEEN EMERGENT READER LIBRARIES®

BOOSTERS

The Literacy Revolution Continues with
New TERL Booster Titles!

Each Sold Individually

EMERGE [1]

9781680211542

9781680211139

9781680211528

9781680211153

9781680211122

ENGAGE [2]

9781680211146

9781680211337

9781680211290

9781680211535

9781680211313

EXCEL [3]

9781680211306

9781680211320

NEW TITLES COMING SOON!
www.jointheliteracyrevolution.com